KV-513-107

Richmond upon Thames Libraries

Renew online at www.richmond.gov.uk/libraries

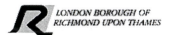
LONDON BOROUGH OF
RICHMOND UPON THAMES

SUNSHINE
STABLES

Have you read?

POPPY *and the* PERFECT PONY
SOPHIE *and the* SPOOKY PONY
GRACIE *and the* GRUMPY PONY
JESS *and the* JUMPY PONY

Coming soon:
WILLOW *and the* WHIZZY PONY

SUNSHINE
STABLES

AMINA *and the*
AMAZING PONY

OLIVIA TUFFIN

ILLUSTRATED BY
JO GOODBERRY

nosy crow

FOR MAURICE

First published in the UK in 2022 by Nosy Crow Ltd
The Crow's Nest, 14 Baden Place, Crosby Row,
London, SE1 1YW, UK

Nosy Crow Eireann Ltd
44 Orchard Grove, Kenmare,
Co Kerry, V93 FY22, Ireland

Nosy Crow and associated logos are trademarks and/or registered
trademarks of Nosy Crow Ltd

978 1 78800 973 7

A CIP catalogue record for this book will be available from the British Library.

CHAPTER 1

"A riding school *team*? Like a proper team? At a show?"

Amina leaned over the side of her camp pony, Nutmeg, to hear a little better. She almost fell right off in excitement, and was saved by her friend Willow grabbing her arm and pulling her back. Lainey, the riding instructor standing in the middle of the arena, chuckled.

"That's right," Lainey said. "A Sunshine Stables team."

Amina wiggled back into her saddle with a grin.

"It sounds a-mazing," she said, looking at her

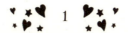

friends who were all gathered round her looking equally excited. They'd just had a brilliant jumping lesson, and then Lainey had called them all into the middle of the arena. "How do we try out?"

"Well," Lainey looked thoughtful. "In a day or so I'll hold a little trial. I've already got four members who are regulars, so it was only fair to offer them a place. But I've got a remaining spot, and would love one of you camp members to fill it!"

There was a buzz of chatter and Amina looked around her happily. She was already having the best ever time at Sunshine Stables pony camp. It was held at the local riding school, Vale Farm, which Lainey owned. And now it was about to get even better!

The riding school was a slice of pony heaven just outside town – lovely old brick stables, and a cobbled yard with chickens scratching about, a pet sheep and paddocks full of the most gorgeous ponies. A few years previously, Lainey had come up with the brilliant idea of running camps for children who didn't have their own ponies, so they could look after one of the school's ponies as if he or she was their very own for a whole week.

Amina had been paired with Nutmeg, one of Vale Farm's tiniest residents. But just like Amina, what she lacked in height, she more than made up for in sparkly personality!

"It sounds great," Jess, one of Amina's friend's, said. "But I'll sit this one out, if that's OK."

Lainey gave her a kind smile. Jess had just helped rescue a beautiful pony called Bandit, who needed some rehabilitation following a diagnosis of stomach ulcers. She was riding another pony called Sorrel in the meantime, but Amina knew she would rather wait her turn to ride Bandit with whom she'd formed a strong bond.

But instead of feeling sad, Amina realised she felt relief that Jess, one of the best riders at camp, had already been eliminated from the competition.

"Of course," Lainey said warmly. "You and Bandit will have your turn soon." She clapped her hands. "So, Jess aside, who's up for trying?"

Everyone else's hand shot up, including Willow's, Poppy's, Sophie's and Gracie's, all Amina's best camp friends alongside Jess. In a short space of time, the girls had already had loads of adventures! They'd bonded on their first day, after finding an old horseshoe under the oak tree in the yard and hanging it up above their camp beds in the barn where they all slept. Amina knew they'd remain good friends, especially as some of them were going to be carrying on with riding lessons at Vale Farm, or helping there on Saturday mornings.

"Me!" Sophie yelled. She rode a gorgeous but cheeky Exmoor called Gorse. Sophie was the joker of the gang, and she and Gorse suited each other brilliantly!

"And me!" Gracie grinned, giving her pony, Bobby, a pat. Gracie and Bobby had got off to a tricky start but, after bonding over a lost kitten, were now the best of friends. Amina knew it would be a chance for Gracie to show everyone how far they'd come. Amina felt the first twinge of real competition, and the excitement faded, just a little.

"I'd love to," Poppy said shyly, and everyone smiled. "I know Henry will look after me." She gave her dark-bay pony a hug. With his bristly mane and heavy hooves, Henry wasn't the flashiest pony, but he was one of the camp stars, kind and trustworthy and talented too.

"Definitely," Willow piped up. "As long as speed is involved, Luna and I will be there!" Willow was an amazing runner, and Luna was a whizzy games pony. It was really clever, Amina marvelled, how Lainey just knew who to match each rider with. She reached forward and gave Nutmeg a hug. *Just like me and Nutmeg*, she thought. *We're* perfect *together.*

Apart from Jess, everyone wanted to try out. Amina gazed around the group, feeling the twinge of competition growing stronger.

"Wonderful!" Lainey smiled at each and

every rider, as they all sat up a little straighter. "If you make the team, we'll travel by horse-box to Wood Plains showground, where we'll compete against other riding schools from the area. There's dressage and stable management in the morning. But the big event is always the showjumping in the afternoon. It's very exciting – loads of thrills and spills! I've seen teams move up from tenth place to win based on the showjumping."

Amina was already lost in thought. She imagined loading Nutmeg up into Lainey's smart blue horse-box in a green rug with matching leg bandages. She'd be wearing a tracksuit over her cream jodhs to keep them clean, and then when she showjumped, she would have a navy jacket with sparkly buttons like her showjumper hero Devon Jenkins wore at competitions.

She imagined riding onto the green turf of the showjumping arena, Nutmeg wearing a Sunshine Stables saddle pad, flying over the coloured poles, her turns sharper and faster than anyone else, her teammates cheering her on as she jumped the last in record time. She'd win the event for them! Then finally, a big red rosette, and cantering around in a lap of honour.

"And remember," Lainey continued. "It's meant to be fun. So don't get worried, and don't take it too seriously."

But Amina *was* taking it seriously. Everyone wanted that place. But *no one* wanted it more than Amina. This was her big chance to prove it had all been worth it.

CHAPTER 2

The team event was still the talk of the yard as the camp members untacked their ponies after the lesson. Everyone was chatting happily as saddles were hung up, hay nets refilled and water buckets fetched to sponge down hot ponies. Amina listened intently as the conversation flew back and forth over the cobbles.

"I'd love to be in the team," Willow sighed as she picked up a sweat scraper. "I've been in teams at area athletics and it's brilliant, but a riding team would be even better."

"My cousin's got a navy jacket," Poppy said,

wiping her bit with a cloth. "I think my auntie would post it. She got all this posh riding gear, and then gave up. Can you *imagine*?"

"I wonder how high the jumps are?" Sophie, who was making rather a lot of mess with a water bucket, said with a grin. "Enormous I bet."

Poppy paled a bit, and stroked Henry.

"Hopefully not too big," she said, sounding nervous.

"They won't be too big," Jess said kindly. "You heard what Lainey said – it's meant to be fun."

"What about you, Amina?" Gracie was leading Bobby back into his stable. "Are you and Nutmeg going for it?"

"A million per cent," Amina said, and it must have sounded really passionate because all the girls looked at her. "I mean, yes, defo. We all are, aren't we?"

"Well, I think we need to make a deal," Willow

said. "There's only one place, right?" Everyone nodded. "Only *one* of us will get to go to the show. We need to promise that whatever happens we'll still all be friends!"

"Of course!" Poppy looked a little confused. "Why wouldn't we be?"

"Oh," Willow said, and Amina wondered if she had glanced at her as she said it, or was that her imagination? "I've seen it at my running club. If someone doesn't get picked for areas or whatever, some people fall out."

"I think it's a good idea," Sophie said, sounding quite sensible, for Sophie. "We all want the place. But we're already having a great time at camp and it would be really sad if anything spoiled that."

"I agree," Jess said. "I know I'm not taking part, but Willow's right."

"Why don't we promise on the horseshoe?" Poppy said in an excited voice. "Make a pact?"

"Perfect!" Sophie grinned. "Come on, the ponies are done. Let's go!"

And everyone raced towards the camp barn, laughing as they ran. Amina followed them. She *knew* Willow was right. They were having a brilliant time at camp, and she'd made such good friends. And the team event *was* meant to be a bit of fun. But still, there was only one place. And she wanted it. More than the others, she thought.

Poppy reached up for the horseshoe, carefully unhooking it. The horseshoe was even more special now the girls knew the history behind it. It had belonged to Lainey's old pony Rosie, who had died almost thirty years ago, shortly after giving birth to her foal, Fable.

Fable still lived out in the paddock by the yard. She was the sweetest grey Welsh pony with a pink snip between her nostrils. She belonged to Lainey's daughter, Emily. Emily was very different from her twin brother, Jack, who was friendly and helpful, but despite Emily's snooty personality, everyone knew she was devoted to Fable. Emily had also recently helped secure Bandit, the new pony, a future on the yard, and was starting to show a softer side.

"Come on," Poppy held the horseshoe out. "Let's do this."

The girls crowded round, each placing a finger on the worn metal of the shoe. Amina did so too, closing her eyes. All she could think about was that final fence in a nail-biting jump-off, the roar of the crowd, Nutmeg's pricked ears and all her family cheering her on.

Willow was talking now, and Amina was jolted back to the present.

"We promise not to let the competition break up our friendship," Willow said. "Let's promise to cheer on the girl who gets the place, whoever that is! Ponies *for ever.*"

"Deal!" Sophie grinned.

"Deal!" Poppy chipped in.

"Definitely," Gracie said with a big smile.

"I'll promise too," said Jess. "I'll cheer you *all* on."

"I promise too," Willow said, then looked at Amina. For a second, Amina's thoughts drifted back to that winning moment in her daydream, her parents' smiles, her sister's cheers. Then she smiled.

"Deal," she said. "Nothing will come between us!"

But even as she said those words, she knew she was going to do everything she could to get that precious place.

With the others still sitting around the camp barn, reading pony magazines and eating sweets from a tuckbox stash, Amina slipped back out to the stables, pausing to stroke Mini the sheep on the way. Nutmeg was in one of the newer stable blocks, and Lainey's husband had made her a special small door so she could see over. A Welsh-Shetland cross, Nutmeg was barely eleven hands high. She was a beautiful golden palomino with a cream-coloured mane and tail.

Lainey had told Amina how she had come across the little pony. "I went to an auction, to buy some tack," she had explained. "And all I could hear was this loud whinnying. It was like she was

shouting for me! I didn't need any more ponies, so I tried to ignore it, but she was so insistent. I came round the corner expecting to see an enormous horse – she was making so much noise – but saw this tiny, scruffy pony. She was the foal of a Welsh Mountain mare crossed with a rogue Shetland and had ended up at the auction. She

was so friendly, I knew I had to take her home."
She grinned. "Plus, she was giving everyone such
a headache that I got her super cheap. And she's
turned into this star."

Nutmeg *was* a star, and she and Amina had
clicked from the word go. The little palomino
made Amina feel like she could jump the moon, a
feeling she hadn't felt in a while…

CHAPTER 3

Amina stroked Nutmeg, the trial still the only thing on her mind. Amina was very close to her parents and big sister, Prisha. They were kind and supportive, but they were also a high-achieving family. She and Prisha had been determined to be top gymnasts. It had meant early-morning starts to get to the gym, long evening training sessions, weekends spent driving to every corner of the country to compete. Until *that* day.

Amina still didn't like to think about it. They'd been taking part in a big regional competition. Prisha had just won her section. All eyes had then been on Amina, to see if they could make it a double victory. It had been going well, until that final ring. Amina could still remember the way her hands had grasped at nothing, the gasp of the crowd, and tumbling through the air before the crack, and the worst pain ever.

But even after her broken ankle had healed, Amina had never gone back to gymnastics. Her family had tried to encourage her, but she didn't want to do it. She'd gone to cheer on Prisha at competitions, but it felt like a different world now, one she no longer belonged to. Truthfully, as time went by, she'd realised she'd never really loved gymnastics, and this had been confirmed the first time her mum had taken her along to a riding stables to cheer her up.

The smell of the hay, the warmth of the ponies' coats and the way they responded when she patted them – it was like she was home. This was what she loved! And she'd never looked back. Although there was that tiny part of her that longed to prove she had been right to have made such a drastic change.

Recently, every evening had been dominated by chatter about Prisha's trip to Germany to compete in a big gymnastics tournament. Amina knew her family hadn't meant to leave her out, and every now and again her sister would slip her hand into hers.

"You OK, Mina?" Prisha would whisper, and Amina would nod. She loved her sister, and she was really proud of her. She didn't want to go to Germany, not one little bit. But that little spark was starting to come back, the flicker of competitive spirit. She wanted *her* thing. So she had been really excited when, one Saturday after her regular riding lesson at a different stables, her mum had taken her to meet Lainey at Vale

Farm, and explained she had booked her on to Sunshine Stables' popular pony camp for a week in the summer.

Amina wasn't sure if she'd done it on purpose, but her mum had chosen the same week Prisha would be in Germany. Her sister was going with her teammates and coach, her first trip abroad without her mum and dad, and Amina hadn't really decided how she was going to spend the week on her own. Camp would be the best sort of distraction: a whole week of pony fun, looking after gorgeous Nutmeg, and making new friends.

But now, with the added excitement of a possible riding-school team place, the little spark had grown into a fire. She knew Prisha was going to do brilliantly. And how cool would it be if she came home with her *own* big success story!

Slipping Nutmeg's head collar on, Amina led the little palomino out into the yard. She selected a soft brush from her grooming kit and used it to bring up a shine on Nutmeg's golden coat. She'd already groomed her that morning, but Amina was determined that Nutmeg should look her very best for the trial. She knew from years of gymnastics that presentation made her feel more confident, and confidence meant she did better. But she had to go beyond just extra grooming for the trial. She needed to look professional!

AMINA *and the* AMAZING PONY

Amina was good at plaiting, but she knew with practise she would be even better, so rather than lounge around reading *Pony* magazine, she decided her time would be best spent perfecting her turnout. Parting Nutmeg's mane, she deftly started to plait, keeping the hair tight and neat, before folding it up. As it was only a trial run for the big day, she used some rubber plaiting bands from her grooming kit, but she made a note to ask Zoe for some cream thread and a needle for the real thing, so her plaits would look even better.

Apple in hand, Poppy wandered out, stroking her favourite ponies, Henry and Misty, along the way, before feeding Henry her apple core and giggling as he smacked his bristly lips.

"What are you doing?" Poppy came over to see Amina, looking with interest over her shoulder. Her gaze fell on the four plaits Amina had now completed.

"Oh," Amina said. "Nothing really."

"Wow!" Poppy said, sounding genuinely impressed. "Amina, those are amazing! Like you'd see at a posh show!"

"Thanks," Amina muttered. "I learnt hair stuff when I was doing gymnastics. It's not so different on a pony."

"You're so clever," Poppy continued wistfully. "I wish I was good at plaiting. It's like I get halfway through and it all goes crazy and they look like big fat lumpy golf balls."

"I'm sure they're OK," Amina said reassuringly.

"Are you plaiting for the trial?" Poppy asked, and Amina nodded after a second's hesitation.

"Yes, maybe, I don't know," she said.

"Perhaps I'll give it a try then," Poppy said. "I want Henry to look his best."

Poppy was so nice and so sweet and Amina

knew she wasn't hinting for Amina to help her, but she *should* offer. She bit her lip and there was a few seconds' silence as she dithered. If it wasn't the trial … she would … she would totally plait Henry up herself.

"I'm sure Henry's mane will look lovely just brushed," she said instead. "And it doesn't matter about the plaits – they will look fine whatever you do. Like Lainey said, it's just a bit of fun. You don't *need* to plait."

Poppy smiled, pushing a strand of her pale hair back.

"You think?" she said. And Amina nodded.

"Definitely," she replied, any guilty feelings trickling away. It was just plaits, she told herself. It didn't *matter*. It would be all about the riding. And if she helped Poppy, then everyone would want help, and if she plaited up everyone else's ponies, she wouldn't be taking this trial seriously. And it meant more to her than anything right now!

CHAPTER 4

All that was left of Amina's plaiting practice a short while later was a slight curl in Nutmeg's creamy mane as Amina tacked her up ready for the afternoon lesson.

"That's it, have a walk around!"

Lainey was in the middle of the arena as the camp members filed through the gate. Sophie and Gorse were in front of Amina and Nutmeg, and Gorse was cheerfully mooching along, his fluffy Exmoor ears pricked. But he kept stopping to gaze at his pony friends in the paddock and Sophie kept laughing. Amina swallowed a wave of irritation.

Every time Gorse stopped, Nutmeg had to stop too, and her nice rhythm was interrupted.

"I'm coming past," Amina said as Gorse stopped again. It must have sounded snappier than she meant it to because Sophie looked round in surprise as Amina nudged Nutmeg on round Gorse's dappled bottom.

"Sorry," Sophie called, but Amina was already riding Nutmeg into an active, swinging walk. Despite her size, Nutmeg had beautiful paces which, combined with her golden palomino colouring, meant she was a real showstopper. And now she wasn't stuck behind Gorse's fluffy behind, it meant Amina could really catch Lainey's eye. She wanted Lainey to be seriously considering her for a place before she even got to the trial. *Every* ride counted.

"It's OK," she called back to Sophie, hoping

her friend wasn't put out. "It's just that Gorse kept stopping and Nutmeg was getting a little annoyed."

Well, I was getting annoyed, she thought. But she didn't say that.

"Yeah," Sophie gathered her reins and nudged the Exmoor on. "He just likes to have a look at

everything." She didn't sound upset and gave Amina a big grin as Amina glanced back.

"Nutmeg looks nice," Sophie added and Amina felt herself swell with pride. She knew she was a naturally talented rider and was so pleased Lainey had paired her with an equally talented pony. She made sure she spent the rest of the lesson in Lainey's full view.

Sometimes it meant she had to overtake the other ponies. Poppy good-naturedly moved Henry aside, as if aware his slow steady strides were no match for Nutmeg's paces. But Willow gave Amina a bit of a look as she came past. Luna was equally quick, but Amina wanted Lainey to get a really good view of Nutmeg's extended trot.

"Sorry, am I holding you up?" Willow muttered and Amina noted the slightest edge to her voice, but she was too caught up in the amazing feeling of Nutmeg's trot to worry too much. She gave the little palomino a pat as they finished up, walking around the sand on loose reins. It had been a great lesson, Amina thought happily. Lainey was *bound* to have noticed how good she and Nutmeg looked.

But Lainey praised them all equally, from Poppy's hesitant canter, to Jess's sitting trot. She told Amina that Nutmeg's figure of eight had been really good, but she certainly hadn't singled her out for extra compliments. Amina slumped in the saddle. She'd really wanted to make a great impression. She would have to up her game!

"Now." Lainey grinned round at the group. "Enough of the serious stuff. What about some handy pony?"

There was a ripple of excited chatter.

"Yes, yes!" Sophie cried.

Willow laughed. "Defo!"

Everyone seemed really up for it. But no one

had noticed that Amina hadn't put her hand up.

She didn't want to do handy pony. She'd hoped for some jumping, or even another flatwork lesson. She thought about Prisha in Germany. She bet she wasn't having any sort of fun and games – it would be training, and that's it. That's how they got their results. She wanted her own success. That's what they were known for, her and Prisha. Success.

But Lainey was already leading the way over to the little field next to the arena, where a handy-pony course had been set up. There was everything from a washing-up bowl full of plastic ducks and a fishing net to hook them out with, a mock washing line with socks ready to peg up, and a flag to move from cone to cone. Everything had to be done from the pony's back, and it was against the clock too.

But to Amina, it just looked like a waste of

time, especially when she looked over to the arena, where the brightly coloured showjumps lay invitingly to the side, ready to be put up. She made a face, and it must have been obvious because Jess looked over at her.

"What's up?" Jess asked, giving Sorrel, the pony she was riding today, a pat.

Amina hesitated. She didn't really want to tell Jess why she was annoyed at having to take part in the handy-pony challenge, because then Jess would know how seriously Amina was taking the trial. If everyone knew, they'd put more effort in too.

"Oh," she said. "Just a bit of a headache."

Jess looked concerned.

"Do you want me to ride back to the stables with you?"

Amina shook her head.

"No," she said. "That's OK. I'll be fine."

SUNSHINE STABLES

She wasn't sure if Jess completely believed her, but they were all lining up now, ready to take their turn. Sophie was up first, and reduced everyone to fits of laughter as Gorse rolled his eyes and refused to go near the fishing net. Finally, Sophie grabbed it, but she was giggling so hard she totally failed to hook a duck and plopped gently out of the saddle instead, landing on the soft grass and shrieking with hysterical laughter. Lainey helped her up onto Gorse's wide, dappled back, Sophie still clutching the dreaded fishing net.

"Come on, Sophie," Lainey said in a mock stern voice, trying to control her own giggles. "Don't you know this is the Handy-Pony Olympics?!"

Poppy fared better on reliable Henry who was totally unfazed by everything! He positioned himself perfectly so Poppy could

work her way through all the obstacles, even standing under the flapping washing line so she could peg up the socks. Willow's Luna was superfast but spooked at everything in dramatic fashion, making everyone fall about laughing again.

"It's not as easy as it looks, is it?" Lainey called, a big grin on her face as Willow cantered Luna over the finishing line. "Nothing tests your riding like a handy-pony course."

"Definitely not! I think this is my favourite lesson so far!" Willow gave Luna a big hug. "Go on, Amina, your turn."

But Amina didn't want to go. How could she show off her best riding to Lainey while hooking plastic ducks and carrying a flag around? She squashed down the small voice inside her that said she would normally love this sort of thing, that it would be a real laugh.

But compared to riding in a team around a showjumping course, it just seemed so ... *babyish*. And how could it test her riding as Lainey said? It was just playing silly games!

CHAPTER 5

But everyone was looking at Amina now and she had no choice. Nudging Nutmeg on, she rode up to the bending poles. She had to move an upturned mug from the first to the last pole, and did so without any problem. The stepping stones were easy – Amina was naturally balanced and wasn't fooling around like the others so did them in double quick time.

But she came unstuck at the fishing net. Nutmeg would *not* go near it! Amina could feel a bubble of frustration rise in her. To think they could be training, or even watching videos of

Lainey riding around Badminton for inspiration, but instead she was stuck here, trying to fish for stupid ducks with a stupid net.

"Come on, Nutmeg." Amina patted her. "I don't want to be here either. Let's just get it over with."

She glanced over at her friends, but she noticed they weren't laughing like they had been with Sophie and Willow. Actually, Jess looked really thoughtful. Amina wondered if her friend knew what she was thinking – Jess always seemed to notice things. She reached over to grab the net and, putting all her weight onto her right foot as she leant over the saddle, felt herself toppling towards the ground as Nutmeg darted sideways.

She fell onto the soft grass as gently as Sophie had, completely unhurt. But *she* didn't see the funny side. Crossly, she got up, and dusted herself down, giving Nutmeg a reassuring stroke to let her know she was OK.

"Oh dear!" Lainey called over. "Do you want to try again?"

"I'll sit this one out," Amina muttered, hopping back into the saddle. "Please."

"Oh, OK!" Lainey said, but she seemed to look at Amina with the same thoughtful expression as Jess. "Why don't you give it a try, Gracie?"

"You bet!" Gracie grinned, nudging Bobby, her handsome piebald, forward. "Cheer me on, you guys!"

Everyone whooped as Gracie attempted the course, but Amina felt the mood had changed a bit, like she'd slightly spoilt the fun. She felt really bad.

But at the same time she had come to the conclusion no one was taking the trial seriously. No one wanted the team place as much as she did. And no one *needed* it as much as she did either.

"Hey, Amina?"

Jess was the first to catch up with Amina as she put Nutmeg back into her stable and hung up her tack. She was just heading over to the barn with Nutmeg's hay net when Jess fell into step beside her.

"Are you OK?" Jess asked.

Amina nodded.

"I'm fine!" she said, hoping she sounded cheerful. "It was just a headache."

"Oh," Jess sounded doubtful. "We all thought ... well ... we just thought you looked like you weren't enjoying yourself."

"I was," Amina said. "But..." She paused. Jess seemed like she might understand. "Don't you think we should be training instead? With the trial coming up?"

But Jess, now holding the barn door open for Amina, just looked at her in astonishment.

"But this is what camp is about!" she said. "It's

fun. Not a training camp? We do enough serious stuff at school!"

Amina was torn. It was fun, and she'd been having the best time ever, until Lainey had mentioned the team trial. Then *everything* had changed. She thought again of Prisha in Germany.

"I guess," she said. "You're probably right." But she could tell Jess wasn't convinced. For a few minutes, they stood in silence, stuffing their hay nets with the sweet-smelling meadow hay. It was one of Amina's favourite smells and she took a deep breath, inhaling it. It reminded her of the simple joy of being around horses.

"Tell you what," Jess then said with a smile. "We're going up to the top field to play rounders. There are no ponies up there at the moment." She linked her arm through Amina's as they walked back to the stables. "Come on up – let's have a laugh."

Amina knew it would be. All her friends, up in the field in the warm sunshine. But at that moment, something caught her eye. Jade, Vale Farm's young riding instructor, was cantering her gorgeous grey gelding, Sox, around the arena in a quiet moment between lessons.

Amina stared, transfixed by Jade's light hands and the way she barely seemed to move in the saddle. Suddenly Amina just wanted to stay and watch. It would make up for missing any training during the handy-pony session.

"Actually," she said, putting her hand to her forehead in what she hoped was a convincing manner, "I still don't feel great. I think I'll sit on my bed for a bit."

Jess shrugged.

"Sure," she said. "I hope you feel better soon."

There was something odd about Jess's tone, but Amina couldn't quite work out what it was.

"Thank you," Amina replied. "If I rest now, then I'll be good for the cross-country walk."

Later on that afternoon, Lainey was going to take the camp members out on foot around the cross-country course to talk them through the dos and don'ts of rustic fence riding. Amina knew it was called a "course walk" and she was looking forward to it. She was determined to soak up every piece of information she could between now and the trial.

When she was quite sure Jess was out of sight, right up at the top of the farm in the big field, Amina padded quietly out to sit on the daisy-covered bank that ran around the edge of the arena.

She could hear the distant shouts of laughter from what sounded like a fun game of rounders and felt a little wistful. She wanted to be up there too. But it was short-term pain for long-term gain, that's what her gymnastics coach used to say. Once she had her team place, she could enjoy camp again. After all, they'd all made a promise on the horseshoe to support whoever got the place, hadn't they?

Jade was popping over some big showjumps now. Her ponytail swung out behind her as she cantered down, the pink and white poles disappearing under Sox's hooves. It was lovely to watch. Giving Sox a big pat, Jade let him walk around the arena on a loose rein, then she gave a start as she seemed to notice Amina for the first time.

"Hey!" Jade waved. "I didn't realise you were

here. I get so caught up in it all. Good boy, Sox."

"You looked amazing," Amina said. "I was watching to see if I could pick up some tips."

"Ah, the team trial?" Jade said. "That's a good idea."

She jumped off Sox and led him over.

"Do you want me to lunge you on him?" she said, and Amina's mouth fell open. Jade laughed. "He's super safe, I promise. He's a schoolmaster."

"Wow!" Amina said, leaping to her feet. "Yes, please!" What an opportunity!

"Let me go and get his lunging stuff," Jade

continued. "Tell you what, go and ask the others if they'd like a go too. A lunge lesson would be great for your position – perhaps I can give you all some tips before the trial."

Amina nodded, and headed off to the big field as Jade led Sox to his stable, preoccupied with kitting him up for the lunge. But as Amina rounded the hay barn and looked up towards the paddocks, her steps slowed. She could see her friends up there, all running around, shrieking with laughter. Sophie had just hit the ball and it had gone right across the field. Willow and Poppy were sprinting after it in hot pursuit.

Jess said they were having a fun game, she told herself. *I'm sure they won't want to be interrupted.*

She twisted her hands round, feeling a little sick. But she'd stopped now, and her feet were no longer taking her in the direction of the field. Instead she counted to one hundred, very slowly, before heading back into the yard.

It's only five minutes on a lunge line, she thought. *They probably wouldn't want to stop playing.* But she felt a huge wave of guilt. She knew it was wrong of her.

CHAPTER 6

"Just you?" Jade said cheerfully, and Amina nodded.

"They're playing rounders," she said. She chewed on her thumbnail, hoping Jade wouldn't clock her guilty face. But Jade laughed.

"Camp tradition!" she said. "No matter, I'll have time later in the week for everyone."

And before Amina knew it, she was up in Sox's saddle. The ground seemed a long way down, but there was something about Sox's calm nature and big grey ears that made her feel really safe. He responded to Jade's voice commands, and after a couple of circles of walking, powered forward into the most beautiful trot. Amina felt as though she was floating, and with Jade holding on to the lunge line, it meant she could really concentrate on keeping her heels down, and her hands light, trying to copy the way Jade rode.

"Lovely!" Jade called from the middle. "Would you like to try a canter?"

Her dark plait bobbing in time to Sox's trot, Amina grinned back.

"Yes, please!"

"OK!" Jade said. "And can-ter."

And just like that, Sox was cantering, the most collected, powerful canter Amina had ever ridden. It was the best feeling in the world! For a few minutes, everything melted away, until it was just her and Sox, and nothing else mattered.

"And walk, and wa-lk," Jade said, breaking through Amina's thoughts. "That was brilliant,

Amina. Try and keep that same position on the trial day, and you should do really well!"

"Do you think?" Amina said, totally thrilled by Jade's compliment, and Jade nodded.

"Yes, absolutely," she said. "But try not to let it worry you. What will be, will be. It's fun."

"But what if I really, *really* want it?" Amina blurted out, and Jade looked up in surprise.

"It clearly means a lot to you," she said. "But

it wouldn't be the end of the world if you didn't make the team, would it?"

"It would feel like it," Amina muttered. And before she could stop herself, she had told Jade all about Prisha, out in Germany.

"So you see," Amina said, "everyone wanted me to go back to gymnastics. They said I could have been a champion if I had just stuck to it. But when I first came to the stables, I knew I loved ponies more than anything. But I wanted to *show* everyone that it was right, me switching from gymnastics to ponies."

Jade gently placed a hand on Amina's arm.

"Amina," she said. "You don't need rosettes and team places to prove that." She gave Sox a pat. "I promise you."

But there was no time to talk to Jade any more. Amina gave Sox a big hug, breathing in his lovely warm horse scent. Sliding off his back, she turned in horror as she heard a familiar cheerful babble of voices. Her friends were skipping back into the yard clutching juice cartons, their faces rosy and happy.

"Oh cool!" Sophie bounded over. "Did you ride Sox?"

"Yes," Amina said, trying not to catch Jess's eye. She'd told Jess she hadn't been feeling well. "Only for a few minutes."

"He's lovely!" Poppy sighed. "Lucky you, Amina."

Jade, gathering up the lunge line, smiled.

"I'll make sure you all have a turn by the end of the week," she said. "Sox will enjoy it." To Amina's huge relief, she didn't say anything about the rounders game or Amina coming to ask them. *It was fine*, Amina said to herself. *They'll all get a turn, see?* She tried to ignore the guilty voice that told her she'd probably be the only one who got a turn before the trial.

"Come on, Amina!" Sophie nudged her arm. "We're doing the course walk now."

"OK," Amina mumbled. "Let me grab my trainers."

"Oh!" Poppy said. "I didn't bring trainers. Do you think my riding boots will be OK? I've been wearing them all afternoon."

"I'm sure they'll be fine," Amina answered before she could stop herself. "I saw you run pretty fast in them up in the field when I came to ask…" Her voice trailed off, and she coughed, hoping Poppy hadn't noticed. But Willow had.

"What did you come to ask?" Willow said. "I didn't see you."

"I thought you were feeling ill," Jess added.

"It was only to see if you wanted a juice," Amina muttered weakly. "But then I got distracted by Sox. By the time I remembered, you'd already got drinks."

"See you guys later!" Jade called from across the yard, a lunge rope over her shoulder. "I'll try and pick a time when you're not playing rounders."

Both Willow and Jess looked at Amina then, and Amina could tell by their faces they knew she wasn't telling the truth. She felt absolutely awful. They didn't say anything else, but Amina knew she was rumbled. She wished she had just played rounders with them, but at the same time, she was still buzzing inside after that amazing ride with Jade. She felt all confused, torn in different directions, but there was no time to chat to her friends and try and make it up to them. Lainey was calling them over now, ready to start the cross-country course walk.

CHAPTER 7

"OK everyone!" Lainey said as they gathered at the start of the course in between two flags. "Does anyone know what the most important thing to remember is when riding cross-country?"

As everyone shot up a hand, all eager to answer Lainey's questions, Amina looked around. She felt as though she was on the edge of the group at that moment, and it made her sad, even though she knew it was her own doing. Everyone seemed to be avoiding her, and she didn't blame them.

The children jogged alongside Lainey as they walked from jump to jump, discussing how they would approach each one, what they'd look out for and how they'd ride away from it. From the logs, to the tyres, the ditch and the steps, each jump was looked at carefully. The excitement was growing amongst the camp members. Tomorrow, they'd be jumping these for real!

"Now." Lainey grinned as they walked on. "Everyone's favourite coming up! The water jump!" And leading them over, she gestured to the purpose-built water feature.

"Not always the easiest," Lainey continued. "Especially for ponies who are nervous, or fancy a naughty splash!" Then she pulled off her boots. "So when I was walking big courses, I often walked through the water jumps in my wellies, got a feel for how deep they were and what the ground was like, but," she winked at the group, "since it's such a hot day, why don't we have a paddle barefoot?"

Sophie was first to kick her trainers off with a whoop, followed by Poppy, tugging off her dusty jodhpur boots. Both hopped off the rustic step with a splash.

"Come on in!" Sophie cried. "It's lovely. Like paddling in a stream."

Everyone was following them in now, boots and trainers discarded. For a second, Amina hovered. Despite feeling distant from the others, she'd been enjoying the cross-country walk, she'd learnt so much, and she wanted to carry on. But it did look *fun*. She reached down and untied her laces, kicking off her own trainers, and waded into the water, which felt beautifully cool on such a hot summer's day.

"Oh, whoops!" Lainey said with a chuckle, splashing Willow, who screeched with laughter and splashed back, before Sophie, and Poppy, Jess and Gracie did the same. And before she

knew it, Amina was also joining in, hysterical with giggles as the camp members splashed each other, drenching shorts and ponytails.

"This is one of Sunshine Stables' traditions!" Lainey laughed. "Wouldn't be camp without a water-jump water fight."

After everyone was suitably soaked, they clambered out and sat on the grassy bank, quickly drying off in the hot sun.

"I think that was one of the best moments of camp," Sophie said with a grin.

Jess nodded. "Definitely!"

Amina looked around at her friends' happy, sunny faces, full of excitement about a fun day jumping tomorrow. The water fight had been a turning point, she realised. She'd had fun too. She needed to stop thinking about the trial and start enjoying all camp had to offer.

"Come on then." Lainey hopped up. "There are

four more jumps still to look at."

Skipping happily, the camp members followed Lainey as she explained the next two jumps, a palisade and a tiger trap. The palisade was simple enough, a solid sloping timber fence, and despite its scary name, Amina couldn't wait to jump the tiger trap, another sloping fence, but this time open and made up of wooden rails.

"Woo!" Sophie said. "Let's hope there are no real-life tigers in it tomorrow!"

Everyone laughed, and Amina laughed too. It was the best she'd felt in ages.

"I'll make sure there's not, or perhaps just a really little one," Lainey said with a chuckle, gathering everyone around her. "And now we're on the home straight. But you can't relax and think you're done. There's something you've got to watch out for after this jump…" And she strode out five steps after the tiger trap. "You need to be turning left here, even though it's going *away* from home," she explained. "Your pony will want to continue home and you'll be jumping that, before you know it." She pointed and everyone followed her gaze. An imposing set of rails lay in line with the smaller tiger trap they'd just looked at.

"That's one of the senior jumps," Lainey said. "It's your choice, and you can jump it if you want, but I'd recommend you stick to the smaller jump." She pointed to the left. "This is yours."

To everyone's relief, it was an inviting jump made up of straw bales. "Then back up towards the yard, and over that last log," Lainey added. "And done!"

"Phew!" Poppy said. "I don't fancy jumping those enormous rails."

"What would you do if we did?" Sophie added cheekily. "Not that I have any intention of doing so – no, thanks!"

"Well," Lainey said. "If you cleared them nicely, I'd be very impressed! But I don't want anyone doing anything they aren't happy with. Perhaps best to stick to the straw-bale jump. Come on, back to the yard."

As everyone followed Lainey, Amina glanced back at the bigger jump. Everyone seemed to think it was really scary, but Amina thought it looked like a challenge! But remembering her promise to herself to enjoy the moment, after looking back one last time, she ran after her friends, opening her arms in the early evening sunshine.

"Nutmeg!"

Amina bounded up to the little palomino, who greeted her with a snuffly whicker at the field gate, ready for Amina to bring her in for the night after her afternoon out in the field. Slipping her head collar on, Amina gave her a hug, inhaling the wonderful pony scent of her warm coat. It was the best feeling in the world – no pressure, just being with her favourite pony.

"Let's have fun tomorrow, girl," she said. "Just enjoy it."

As she led Nutmeg back into the yard, clip-clopping over the cobbles, Amina gave a start as a familiar car pulled through the gateway. The car parked beside the stable block and a smiling woman climbed out.

"Mum!"

With Nutmeg trotting alongside, Amina hurried over to her mum and threw herself into her arms. She needed a hug after an unsettling day.

"Amina!" her mum said with a smile, reaching into the car for a paper bag. "I've just been over to see your gran and she sent me back with these. I thought you could share them with your friends."

Amina peeked into the bag, and grinned at

the sight of the delicious
barfi, a sweet her
gran made better
than anyone she
knew. They were her
absolute favourite! She
knew her friends would love
them and imagined them
all sitting on hay bales
chatting away and
sharing the sweets. She
knew she hadn't been
a great friend recently.
Hopefully it was a way to show
them she hadn't meant to get
carried away over the trial.

"Thanks, Mum," she said happily.
"How's Gran?"

"She's good," her mum replied. "I wanted to

share the videos of Prisha with her."

Amina thought about her older sister. She missed her loads! And she had to ask, even though she knew it would make her feel a bit funny.

"Is ... is Prisha doing really well?" She swallowed, even though she knew the answer. Pride was written all over her mum's face.

"Well, she's won her section and has made it into the championships," her mum said. "We'll hear about that tomorrow evening before she flies home the following morning."

Then she gave Amina another hug, and Nutmeg a little pat.

"But look at you," she said warmly. "In your happy place, with this lovely pony, and you look so content."

Amina knew she did. Still slightly damp from the water fight, her plait unravelling, a dusting of palomino hairs over her T-shirt and a smudge of slobber on her shoulder where Nutmeg had given her an affectionate nudge. But still, she couldn't shake the feeling that had started to build inside her again, however hard she tried to squash it down. *She* wanted to have good news too. What a day that would be! Prisha in the championships and Amina with a team place. But how could she make that happen? What more could she do to impress Lainey?

CHAPTER 8

Amina had her answer a short while later. Emily, Lainey's daughter, wandered past on her way to give Fable a groom. Emily had been really moody at the start of camp, and Amina knew she could be funny about strangers looking after the school ponies. But she had warmed to the group after helping Jess with Bandit.

"Hey, Amina." Emily waved, pausing by Nutmeg's stable door, where Amina was just finishing off tidying up her shavings bed. "How was the course walk?"

"It was good," Amina said. "I'm looking

forward to jumping it!"

"You know Nutmeg's a cross-country star?" Emily continued. "She can jump the big course. She's done loads of cross-country competitions too."

Amina stopped sweeping, and stood perfectly still as she took this in.

"Wow!" she said. "Really?"

Emily nodded.

"Yeah," she replied. "Actually, hang on a sec. I've got some really cool photos that Mum bought from the professional photographers."

Amina tapped her fingers against the handle of the brush impatiently as Emily sprinted towards the house. Nutmeg was munching hay next to her, her golden coat catching the evening sun. Soon Emily returned, clutching an envelope.

"Look," Emily said, drawing out several photographs. "This is Maddie, a girl who rides for mum sometimes. She's small so can ride Nutmeg even though she's nearly a grown-up."

Amina stared at the photos. Nutmeg looked amazing in some cool mint-green boots and matching numnah, the girl riding her in a coordinating hat silk, as they soared over some big jumps. Flicking through the photos, her heart flipped. She knew that jump. It was the rails, the last jump Lainey had shown them on the course walk. And there was little Nutmeg, soaring over them, her creamy tail flying behind her, neat ears pricked, and still clearing

the imposing jump with inches to spare.

"Wow!" Amina showed Nutmeg the photo. "Look at you!"

Nutmeg snuffled the photo before carrying on with her hay-munching.

"Cool," Emily grinned. "Isn't it?"

Amina nodded, gazing at the photo again. In her head, she was the girl riding Nutmeg in the mint-green silks, her dark plait flying behind her. She thought about what Lainey had said when Sophie cheekily asked her what she'd do if they jumped the rails.

I'd be very impressed! Lainey's words were whirling around in her head now. Amina had conveniently forgotten the bit where Lainey added that they should probably stick to the smaller jump. No one else had seemed willing to attempt it anyway. And suddenly, Amina knew exactly how to show Lainey what she could do. Something that would prove how brave and talented she was. Why she deserved that team place more than anyone else!

"Oops!" Emily said in a startled voice and Amina looked up. "Look, Mini's out." Emily rolled her eyes. "I'd better go and catch her."

Mini the sheep was making her way in a determined manner to the open door of the feed room, her fluffy tail wiggling as she trotted along with Emily now running behind her, still clutching her envelope of photos. Apart from the one Amina was still holding, of Nutmeg soaring over the rails. Turning it over in her hands, she thought about calling Emily back – she'd now managed to catch Mini. But instead, she tucked it into her T-shirt, vowing to return it the next day.

That night, she slipped it carefully under her pillow, hoping she'd dream of jumping huge fences on her little palomino. Squeezing her eyes shut, blocking out the pony-filled chatter of her friends as they sat crossed legged in their pyjamas, she imagined herself once again, jumping the rails like the girl in the photo. It was only as she finally dropped off to sleep that she remembered the sweets her mum had dropped off. She'd forgotten all about them.

Amina was sure her friends could read her mind the next morning as she dressed ready for the cross-country. Although it wasn't the actual trial, she knew Lainey was going to be watching carefully, so it felt as important. She was quiet and focussed as everyone buzzed and chattered around her. She'd thought she might feel excited, but she felt quite the opposite. She actually longed to sit on the bed with Sophie and Gracie and look through *Pony* magazine, or head down to the stables with Jess to help Jade make up the morning feeds. All the bits she'd loved about camp until Lainey had mentioned the team trial, just hanging out with her friends and caring for the ponies. But she'd made her plan now and she had to give it a try. But did she *actually* want to go through with it? Amina didn't know.

"Are you OK?" Gracie said a little later as they warmed up their ponies in the field next to the cross-country course.

Nutmeg and Bobby were jogging slightly, as if excited by what was to come. Lainey had made the lesson feel super-professional, with stewards, including Jade, and Lainey's husband, standing by the jumps. Lainey was at the end of the course, so she'd have a full view of the last three or four jumps. Jess, Willow and Poppy had already set off and Sophie was at the start, her little Exmoor, Gorse, bouncing about as Lainey's son, Jack, counted them down.

"We noticed you were super quiet after your mum came to visit," Gracie said. "Are you OK?"

Amina gave Nutmeg a pat. It was the first thing anyone had said to her all morning. Amina knew it was her own fault. She'd not said anything either. But Gracie's tone was kind.

"No," she said. "It's not that, it's…" She paused. Amina knew Gracie was a stage actor and singer, and Gracie had told them all about her auditions for London musicals. "Have you ever wanted to prove yourself so badly you…" But then she looked up as Jack waved, interrupting her.

"Your turn next, Amina!"

"Coming!" Amina called back, and gathered up her plaited reins.

"Don't worry," she said to Gracie, who was

struggling slightly to control a bouncy Bobby. "It doesn't matter."

"Amina!" Gracie said. "What do you mean?"

But her words flew away on the breeze as Amina nudged Nutmeg into a trot, heading over to where Jack was standing.

"You're lucky you're on Nutmeg," Jack said with a grin. "She's a cross-country queen!"

Amina smiled back, but her tummy was churning. What *was* she doing?

"Three, two, one," Jack called. "Go!"

And Amina and Nutmeg leapt forward into a speedy canter, towards the first fence, the simple log, which quickly disappeared under Nutmeg's tiny hooves. Her golden ears were pricked forward, her creamy mane was flying and, as she soared over the tyres, the ditch, and then the steps, Amina started to laugh out loud. With the sun shining and Nutmeg's canter striding out over the green turf, it was the very best feeling in the whole world!

Nutmeg was still full of beans as they splashed through the water jump, dampening the underside of her golden tummy and Amina's jodhpurs. On over the palisade, then the last jump before the home straight.

It was now or never. Nutmeg soared over the tiger trap as Amina gripped the reins, closed her eyes for a split second ... and let the little pony head straight on ... towards the rails. Sitting still in the saddle, heels rammed down, hands soft on the reins, sitting, sitting, sitting, then fold! And...

Nutmeg soared over the rails like a bird and Amina felt as though she was truly flying. It was just her and Nutmeg against the world. She wasn't even thinking about the trial, just about how amazing it felt to jump such a

wonderful pony.

"I did it!" she gasped. "I actually did it!"

She was so overcome by the moment that she lost concentration. It was just enough time for Nutmeg, as if elated by the big jump, to start galloping, hurtling towards the next big one on the course, as if saying, *"Hey! I know the way!"*

"Oh, no, Nutmeg!" Amina felt a bubble of panic wipe out the joy. "I only meant that one!"

She had to swing her round quickly. The rails had been one thing, but she didn't fancy jumping the enormous hedge that lay ahead! Tugging desperately on one rein, Amina felt herself lurch sideways as Nutmeg went one way and she went the other. She was aware of hanging in the air for a second before the grass rushed up to meet her and she landed with a thud.

To Amina's relief, Nutmeg came to a halt almost immediately and gave her a nudge as if trying to help her back to her feet, but Amina knew she'd hurt herself. The same ankle! What if it was broken all over again? If she couldn't ride, it would be more than a broken bone. Her heart would be broken!

CHAPTER 9

"Amina!"

Lainey was rushing over, but Sophie was faster. Having handed Gorse's reins to Poppy, she sprinted from where the camp members had been waiting at the end of the course.

"Oh, Amina," Sophie said, crouching down. "What happened?"

Amina wiped away a tear.

"I totally messed up," she whispered. "It's all my fault."

"No, it wasn't." Sophie squeezed her hand. "It was an accident!"

But it had been her fault, Amina knew it. If she hadn't been so determined to impress Lainey and try to win that team place, she would never have attempted the huge fence. No one else had but her. And now she'd lost everything. She'd totally ruined camp!

❤

Amina was still quiet several hours later as she sat up in the cubicle. Lainey had driven her to the emergency department as fast as she could in her rattly old Land Rover, her sweet spaniel dog providing comfort as Amina clutched her soft fur and tried not to cry. It had been awful leaving little Nutmeg, who seemed so worried about her, whinnying madly and dancing about, trying to get back to Amina as Sophie and Jess led her back to the stables. That had been the worst bit of all.

"Hello, young lady!" The smiley nurse who'd seen her earlier when they arrived had popped in. To Amina's huge relief, she had been able to wiggle her toes on the drive to hospital, and the x-rays had shown no breaks. She'd felt really bad for wasting everyone's time, but the doctor had reassured her that they'd always rather check, especially as she'd already broken that same ankle.

"How are you feeling?" The nurse continued. "You may have some bruising, but you should be right as rain before too long. I expect by tomorrow you'll be feeling a lot better."

Tomorrow. The day of the trial. But there was no way Amina would be in with a chance now.

She'd blown it completely. Lainey had had to go back to the stables, but Amina's mum was with her now.

"That's good!" Her mum squeezed her hand. "Do you want to go back to camp?"

Amina didn't. She couldn't face everyone. She should have just enjoyed herself, instead of focussing so much on the trial, but instead she'd behaved really badly. And her friends must know it too. But she missed Nutmeg so much, it hurt!

"No," she mumbled. "Can we go home?"

Amina's mum patted her arm.

"If that's what you really want?" She sounded worried. "I'll let Lainey know. I'll make the phone call, and grab a coffee too."

"Down the corridor on the left," the nurse said cheerily and Amina's mum nodded as she headed towards the door.

"Thank you."

"I hope you'll be back riding soon," the nurse said as Amina's mum left. "It's the only downside of horses, isn't it? The falling off!"

Amina looked at her in surprise. With her red hair pulled back and her sparkly green eyes, the nurse looked fun, but she didn't look much like a horse rider in her neat nurse's uniform.

"But we wouldn't be without them though," the nurse continued cheerfully, topping Amina's water glass up. "Horses, I mean. I have to say, I wish I was young enough to take part in one of those camps of Lainey's. I've often seen groups of youngsters on the beach and in the forest." She paused, and her smile faded. "Wish I'd done that, instead of…" And she shook her head.

"Instead of what?" Amina asked, curious now.

"Well," the nurse said. "I wish I'd just enjoyed being with the ponies. I was a showjumper, you see, and spent the whole time going to events, chasing rosettes. Looking back, I wish I'd just got to live in the moment a little more. Hung out with my pony, ridden with my friends. There's so much more to ponies than winning prizes."

Without her realising it, a tear trickled down Amina's cheek. That had been exactly what she had wanted to do when she first came to camp and before she knew about the trial – just enjoy herself. But she'd still gone ahead with her crazy plan. And now it was too late.

"Hey!" the nurse said, sitting down besides Amina. "I didn't mean to upset you!" She smiled kindly. "Do you want to tell me all about it?"

So Amina did. She told her everything, from her gymnastics injury, to discovering ponies, to wanting to compete with Prisha, and have her own success.

"And the worst thing is," she sniffed as she finished her story, remembering the way she hadn't offered to help Poppy with her mane plaits, and how she had gone behind their backs to have a lunge lesson, "my friends were so nice and I put the trial above them. I've ruined things with them, *and* with Nutmeg."

The nurse patted her arm.

"I'm sure you haven't," she said softly. "Your friends will understand if you tell them exactly what you've told me. And…" She smiled. "The best thing about ponies is they forgive you. Go and see Nutmeg and give her a big hug. It will be the best medicine of all!"

A little later, Amina walked unsteadily out of the hospital entrance. She was right opposite the leisure centre where she used to train, and a few steps away from the little café she and Prisha had gone to after gymnastics. And if you started walking to the left, away from the town, it took you out to the lane that lead back to Sunshine Stables, and her friends, and Nutmeg. More than anything, Amina longed to start running down that leafy lane, straight into the yard and Nutmeg's stable, and to throw her arms around her golden neck, just like the nurse had told her to.

But something was stopping her. She knew she'd let her friends down, going against the pact they had made on the horseshoe and, in doing so, had let Nutmeg down too. She couldn't face everyone.

"Ready, love?" Her mum placed a hand on her

arm. "Are you sure you don't want to go back to camp?"

"I'm sure," Amina said, even though she wasn't sure at all. "My ankle really hurts." It didn't, not much, but Amina needed an excuse. "It would probably be best to just go home."

"OK," her mum said. "If that's what you really want."

Amina nodded, and hung her head, glancing down the lane one last time.

Then she looked again.

A familiar little golden face, a creamy mane and bright, searching eyes. And the pony's leather head collar with the pink lead rope was held by… "Sophie?"

Amina blinked and rubbed her eyes. She wasn't dreaming! There, waiting to cross the road, as the traffic lights turned from green to red, was Nutmeg. And not only was Sophie leading her, but Willow, Jess, Gracie and Poppy were all waiting with her. As the funny little party crossed over, a child waved at them from a car and Sophie waved back.

Amina's throat felt all lumpy, like she might cry, but they were happy tears.

"Sophie!" she repeated. "Poppy, Gracie, Willow and Jess!" She started to walk forward and Nutmeg gave a shrill whinny, practically dragging Sophie the last few steps before Amina threw her arms around the little pony and buried her nose in her soft mane.

"You came to see me," she whispered. "I've missed you so much!"

Then she looked at her friends, her arms still around Nutmeg's neck.

"I ... I don't understand," she said. "You brought Nutmeg to see me, even after I've been so awful this last couple of days."

Poppy smiled kindly.

"When Lainey said you weren't badly hurt but you had decided not to come back to camp, we couldn't understand," she said. "We knew how much you loved Nutmeg, and then, when we were tidying up the camp barn and making your bed, the photo of her jumping that big fence fluttered out."

"We knew you'd been so focussed on that team place," Gracie continued. "But now we know why too. Jade told us a little bit."

Amina hung her head.

"You must think I've behaved so badly," she mumbled. "And we made that pact." She lifted her head and looked straight at her friends. "I'm so sorry."

Then she started to cry.

"Hey!" Willow put her arms around her, as did Jess. "It's OK. We know you got carried away. But we also know you're the best rider! No one else attempted those rails and you did them so amazingly. You *have* to come back to camp and try out."

Nutmeg nudged Amina, and Amina stroked her

golden neck. It felt so good being back with the little palomino.

"No," she said. "I don't want to try out. I got so carried away, I forgot what it was that made me fall in love with ponies in the first place. When I was sitting up there in the hospital after falling off, all I could think about was how much I'd let Nutmeg, and you, down. I should have just enjoyed camp, instead of worrying about proving myself."

"Does that mean you're not coming back?" Poppy asked, sounding upset, but Amina shook her head.

"I'm not going to try out," she said. "But I do really want to come back." She gave Nutmeg a hug. "If that's OK?"

"Hurrah!" Her friends cheered in unison as Amina's mum put her arm around her.

"Well done," she whispered, and Amina smiled.

AMINA *and the* AMAZING PONY

"Can I go back after all, Mum?" she asked, and her mum squeezed her shoulders.

"Of course, my love," she said. "If you're sure your ankle feels OK?"

"Actually," Amina grinned, "it suddenly feels tons better!"

CHAPTER 10

Nutmeg's arrival at the hospital had caused quite a stir, and already the sweet palomino pony was surrounded by people, young and old, from a small girl with a bandaged arm to an old lady with a walking frame. Nutmeg was clearly enjoying the attention.

"Aren't we all going to be in massive trouble?" Amina said nervously to Gracie as she watched several people take out their camera phones. "Lainey's surely going to hear about this!"

But Gracie just smiled, and nudged Amina's arm.

"Look over there," she said. "It was all Lainey's idea."

And Amina looked, and saw Lainey, chatting with the kind nurse from earlier. Both glanced over and waved, before working their way through the group of people gathered around Nutmeg.

"Amina," Lainey said warmly. "I'm so glad you're OK. Emma and I have had the most wonderful idea!"

The nurse, Emma, smiled.

"When I saw you with your lovely pony and how happy she made everyone, I knew I had to ask," she explained. "Lainey has very kindly agreed to bring a pony down here every so often, to come into our garden for the poorly children to stroke."

"It's something I've been thinking about, but I wasn't sure how to go about it." Lainey smiled. "But with us just down the road, it makes perfect sense. The ponies will really enjoy it and if they can help someone in just one small way, well, that would make me very happy indeed."

"They've already helped me." Amina had her arm around Nutmeg as the small crowd started to wander away, back to appointments or waiting taxis. "You were right," she told Emma. "Ponies really are the best medicine!"

Back at Sunshine Stables, it was as though Amina had discovered camp all over again. The simple joy of eating an apple under the oak tree while poring over the pages of *Pony* magazine with her friends. Riding the ponies bareback in from the field (with Lainey's permission), Nutmeg sending up clouds of dust as she trotted down the track. All the pony chores she loved: making sure Nutmeg's water bucket was sparkling, that her saddle was soaped and her creamy mane combed.

Just hanging out in the yard, hearing the happy chatter of everyone around her and soaking up all the pony fun.

The next morning, the camp members had an early hack. Now the pressure to try and impress Lainey was gone, Amina was enjoying her riding again! Just wandering along the bridle path that led out towards the downs felt like the best prize of all. The hedgerows were lush and green and Nutmeg, the smallest, made everyone laugh by trying to sneak huge mouthfuls of grass.

But Lainey had some news for them.

They'd reached a pretty little meadow with a trough for the ponies to have a cool drink from, and as the camp members enjoyed the warmth of the early morning sun on their arms, Lainey turned her horse, Bertie, in front of them and gave him a pat.

"As you know," she said, once she had

everyone's attention. "I was planning on holding a trial this afternoon to find another team member for the show."

She looked around and Amina was suddenly perfectly still, waiting to hear what Lainey might say.

"But," she continued, "on reflection, I've decided to scrap it."

Oh no. Amina's heart thudded into her tummy, her eyes brimming with tears. It was like the sun had gone behind the clouds all of a sudden. She didn't want to try out, but her behaviour meant no one else would get a chance either. She'd ruined it for everyone!

But Lainey was still talking.

"I've looked at the schedule," she said. "And there's absolutely no reason why I can't take two teams. All of you have impressed me with your riding. You did a fantastic job on the cross-country course, but," and she gave the tiniest nod to Amina, "what impressed me most was the way you worked as a team, both on and off your ponies. And I know some lessons were learnt too."

Amina knew Lainey meant her. And she had

definitely learnt her lesson!

"So does that mean we're all going to the show?" Poppy asked, a smile creeping over her face.

"Yes," Lainey said with a laugh. "It might be total chaos, but we'll have fun! And that's the most important bit."

"Who is going to take the place on the other team?" Jess asked.

"Emily," Lainey said, and she looked really pleased. "I know she thinks you've all done amazingly well, and she would love to join in."

Amina knew this was a big step for Emily, who had not liked her mum's decision to change their private stables to a riding school. But now it sounded as though she wanted to get involved, and Amina knew that would mean a huge amount to Lainey. It was brilliant news all round.

"We'll chat it through when we're back,"

Lainey said happily. Then she gestured up the hill, where the meadow opened up. "Now then. There's the most amazing place to canter ahead. Who's up for it?"

And as everyone cheered, nudging their ponies into a walk, then trot, then letting them canter up the hill, Amina felt her heart soar. As Nutmeg thundered on, the wind whipping strands of hair across Amina's face, she laughed with the sheer delight of cantering her favourite pony alongside friends she knew she would have forever.

Amina was still grinning as they clattered into the yard on loose reins, ponies' ears pricked as they looked forward to a washdown and a well-deserved carrot. Then she blinked as she saw a familiar figure rush towards her in the purple tracksuit she used to wear too.

"Prish!" Amina leapt off Nutmeg and gave her

big sister a hug.

Amina's mum was behind her.

"I've just collected Prisha from the airport," she said. "And she was so desperate to see you, I thought we'd swing by."

"Oh, Prisha, it's so nice to see you," Amina said. "How did you do?"

"I got silver," Prisha said proudly. "It was really exciting!"

Amina gave her another hug. She found she didn't actually mind at all. She was just happy for her sister.

"I'm so pleased!"

"But look at you!" Prisha said. "You didn't see us, but we passed you riding down the path, and Mum stopped the car so we could watch. You looked so happy and you're such a good rider! And brave too – I couldn't ride a pony." She gave Nutmeg a cautious pat. "She's so cute."

"Yeah," Amina said happily. "She is. She's the best."

Prisha then reached into her tracksuit pocket and took out her phone, the one she'd got recently, on her thirteenth birthday.

"Can I take a photo?"

And Amina happily obliged, placing her arms around Nutmeg's neck.

"Ah," Prisha said, looking at the screen before turning it round to show Amina. "That's the nicest photo I've ever seen of you. I'll look at it whenever I'm away and missing you."

And Amina looked. Her hair was windswept and she was hot and sweaty, her T-shirt smudged with a green stain from Nutmeg's hedgerow snacks, but all Amina could see was her sparkling eyes and big grin, and the way she was hugging Nutmeg. She felt a warm glow inside. And it was not until a few minutes later, as her mum and Prisha drove out of the yard with a wave, that she realised she hadn't even told them about the show and her team place. It hadn't seemed at all important!

Nutmeg nudged her as if to remind her she'd like her bath now, and laughing, Amina hugged her once again before leading her over to the tie-up area. As she sponged the sweet palomino's golden coat, she grinned at the thought of the rest of camp still to enjoy. And there would be more to come once camp was over. Lainey was going to organise some riding lessons so the teams could practise. But to Amina, that was just more chances to hang out with Nutmeg and her friends.

That had been exactly what Jade meant, she realised. She hadn't needed rosettes or trial success to show that choosing ponies over gymnastics had been the right thing to do. The photo Prisha had taken said it all! Her friends, and Nutmeg, had helped her see that. With her favourite pony by her side, Amina had found her true happiness.

ARE YOU A PERFECT PONY PRO? TAKE THIS QUIZ TO FIND OUT!

1 A FLASH, DROP AND GRACKLE ARE ALL TYPES OF WHAT?

a) Jump

b) Noseband

c) Girth

2 MARES ARE MORE LIKELY TO HAVE FEWER TEETH THAN GELDINGS AND STALLIONS. TRUE OR FALSE?

a) True

b) False

3 WHAT DOES A RED RIBBON IN A PONY'S TAIL MEAN?

a) They are for sale

b) They are a stallion

c) They may kick

4 WHERE MIGHT YOU FIND A SERPENTINE?

a) In a dressage test

b) On a showjumping course

c) On a cross-country course

5 WHAT DOES A FARRIER DO?

a) Looks after your pony's teeth

b) Looks after your pony's feet and shoes

c) A person who clips your pony's coat

**6 WHICH OF THESE IS NOT A
    PONY FACE MARKING?**

a) A blaze
b) A star
c) A moon

7 WHAT IS A FIRST RIDDEN CLASS?

a) A class for young riders
   recently off the lead rein
b) A class for ponies doing their
   first show
c) A gymkhana race